MAX'S LOGBOOK

BY MARISSA MOSS

LOG LIKE TO RECORD SOMETHING, NOT LOG LIKE A PIECE OF WOOD

SCHOOL PHOTO— WHEN THE GUY SAYS "SMILE," I REALLY SMILE!

I THOUGHT I COULD USE TEETH PRINTS AS A SECURITY DEVICE — ONLY PEOPLE WHOSE TEETH MATCH THESE CAN OPEN THIS BOOK, BUT MY OLDER BROTHER, KEVIN, SAID THAT WOULDN'T WORK BECAUSE WHAT HAPPENS WHEN MY BRACES COME OFF?

SCHOLASTIC PRESS • NEW YORK

SO THIS IS MY NEW SECURITY SYSTEM

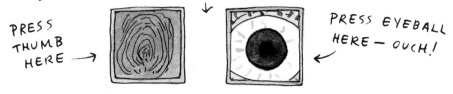

PRESS THUMB HERE →

↓

PRESS EYEBALL HERE — OUCH!

THIS IS MY NEW LOGBOOK FOR WRITING SCIENTIFIC STUFF IN. MY MOM AND DAD ARE REAL SCIENTISTS, AND I'M WORKING ON BECOMING ONE, TOO. I GOT THE IDEA TO START THIS RECORD FROM A GIRL IN MY CLASS WHO KEEPS A NOTEBOOK ABOUT EVERYTHING IN HER LIFE.

SUPER BORING!

I WOULD NEVER, I MEAN NEVER, DO THAT, BUT I HAVE SO MANY GREAT IDEAS, I NEED A PLACE TO RECORD THEM. I DON'T WANT TO FORGET ANY OF MY COOL INVENTIONS OR EXPERIMENTS.

EXPERIMENT # 1:
WHAT HAPPENS WHEN YOU MICROWAVE A MARSHMALLOW?

LITMUS PAPER ↓

TONGS FOR PICKING GREEN THINGS OFF PIZZAS

BUNSEN BURNER ↓

TEST TUBES

AH! THE SMELL OF FRESH-COOKED CHEMICALS →

HER NOTEBOOKS LOOK LIKE THIS. SHE MUST HAVE FILLED UP ABOUT 20 BY NOW!

BEAKERS OF STRANGE POWDERS AND FLUIDS →

MAD SCIENTIST ↓

LIGHTNING BOLT HAIR →

INNOCENT MARSHMALLOW WHOSE ONLY FEARS INVOLVE CAMPFIRES AND GRAHAM CRACKERS. WHAT STRANGE FATE AWAITS YOU?

STAINS FROM CHEMICALS, KETCHUP, AND MUSTARD (NOTHING LIKE A RADIOACTIVE HOT DOG FOR LUNCH!)

HEE, HEE! COME TO ME, MY PRECIOUS SWEET (OR SWEET PRECIOUS)! I AM ABOUT TO TURN YOU INTO...

MARSHMALLOW GOO EXPLODING OUT OF MICROWAVE

1. PUT MARSHMALLOW ON PAPER PLATE INSIDE THE MICROWAVE.
2. SET FOR 40 TO 60 SECONDS.
3. STAND BACK AND WATCH THE AMAZING TRANSFORMATION INTO....

GODZILLA PUFF!

OBSERVATIONS: AFTER 20 SECONDS, THE MARSHMALLOW BEGAN TO PUFF UP. AT 40 SECONDS, IT WAS $\frac{4}{=}$ TIMES BIGGER THAN BEFORE.

MADE WHOLE ARMY OF MUTANT MARSHMALLOWS.

MARSHMALLOW COULD THEN BE SHAPED EASILY.

IT TASTED CRUNCHY, KIND OF LIKE THE CARDBOARDY MARSHMALLOWS IN CEREAL.

THE ZOMBIE

MARSHMALLOW BOY

THE BLOB

MUSHROOMY MALLOW

HORNED MARSHMALLOW

THE GHOST

THE HEADLESS WONDER

RESULTS: ONE ANGRY MOM FOR MAKING A MARSHMALLOWY MESS, BUT WHEN I TOLD DAD ABOUT IT, HE THOUGHT IT WAS COOL.

MAD MOTHER LOOKS KIND OF LIKE MAD SCIENTIST. →

HOW MANY TIMES DO I HAVE TO TELL YOU, THIS IS A KITCHEN, NOT A LABORATORY!

DAD TRIES TO BE THE VOICE OF REASON.
↓

IT'S JUST NORMAL SCIENTIFIC CURIOSITY.

SHOULDN'T WE ENCOURAGE THAT?

I WISH I WAS BETTER AT DRAWING HANDS. I ALWAYS END UP WITH PAWS.

THAT STARTED ANOTHER FIGHT BETWEEN MOM AND DAD. IT SEEMS LIKE THEY'RE ALWAYS FIGHTING THESE DAYS. I STILL **ENDED UP BEING SENT TO MY ROOM,** BUT THAT GAVE ME THE CHANCE TO WORK ON AN INVENTION.

INVENTION #1:
HOW TO MAKE AN ALARM SO IF ANYONE (THAT MEANS YOU, KEVIN, OR MOM, THE SNEAKY ROOM REARRANGER) COMES IN MY ROOM, A LOUD BUZZER GOES OFF

BZZZZZZZZZ

OPENING THE DOOR BREAKS THE CIRCUIT, → CAUSING ALARM TO SOUND.

DOOR JAMB
DOOR →
WIRE
BUZZER
DOORKNOB
BATTERY (TAPED ON)

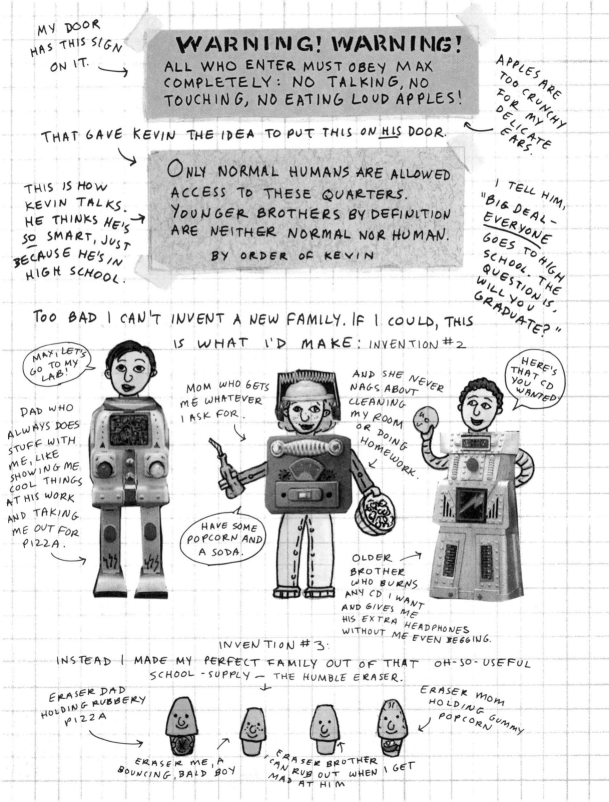

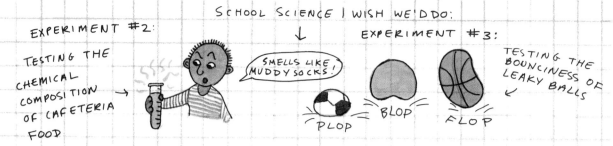

EXPERIMENT #2:

TESTING THE CHEMICAL COMPOSITION OF CAFETERIA FOOD →

SMELLS LIKE MUDDY SOCKS!

EXPERIMENT #3:

TESTING THE BOUNCINESS OF LEAKY BALLS ↙

PLOP · BLOP · FLOP

AT SCHOOL, WE MADE VOLCANOES AGAIN. HOW MANY TIMES DO WE HAVE TO MIX BAKING SODA AND VINEGAR? WHEN DO WE GET TO USE REAL CHEMICALS? DAD SAYS WHEN HE WAS A KID, YOU COULD GET ALL KINDS OF COOL STUFF YOU CAN'T BUY ANYMORE. HE EVEN MADE HIS OWN FIREWORKS.

KABOOM!

EXCEPT ONCE HE BLEW UP THE DRIVEWAY MAKING THEM. I GUESS THAT'S WHY YOU CAN'T BUY THOSE INGREDIENTS NOW.

OMAR WAS MY VOLCANO PARTNER. WE ALWAYS TRY TO BE PARTNERS SINCE WE'RE BEST FRIENDS.

OMAR ALWAYS WEARS A CAP. I USED TO THINK HE WAS BALD. NOW I KNOW HE'S JUST A CAP FREAK— HE HAS 63 DIFFERENT ONES!

EXPERIMENT #4:

PAPER CUP WITH BOTTOM CUT OUT

WAX PAPER RUBBER-BANDED TO SEAL THE TOP

ME WITH VOLCANO INGREDIENTS ↓

VINEGAR

ACTUALLY, THE ERUPTING LAVA REMINDED ME OF MOM AND DAD WHEN THEY'RE FIGHTING. →

MOM →

WHY DO GROWN-UPS FIGHT ANYWAY, AREN'T THEY SUPPOSED TO BEHAVE BETTER THAN KIDS?

← DAD

I WANTED TO MAKE THINGS MORE INTERESTING THAN THE SAME OLD VOLCANO, SO WE MADE A GROUP OF ERASER PEOPLE TRYING TO FLEE THE BURNING LAVA.

SHOCKED, PANICKY ERASER PEOPLE
↓

OMAR LOVED THE IDEA, BUT OUR TEACHER MS. BLODGE DIDN'T THINK IT WAS FUNNY — OR EDUCATIONAL.

ERASERS ARE <u>NOT</u> PART OF THIS EXPERIMENT, BOYS. PUT THEM AWAY NOW...

OR I'LL CONFISCATE THEM!

← JOWLY CHEEKS SO IT LOOKS LIKE SHE HAS 3 CHINS

THE DREADED "C" WORD! MS. BLODGE ALREADY HAS:

MY EXTRA-LARGE RUBBER BAND BALL — IT TOOK A WHOLE MONTH TO MAKE!

MY FLATTENED PENNY, SMUSHED BY THE TRAIN
↓

MY FOLDING COMB THAT LOOKS LIKE A SWITCHBLADE WHEN IT'S FOLDED BUT OPENS INTO A COMB
↓

ERUPTING VOLCANO →

WITHOUT VILLAGERS FLEEING DRAMATICALLY — BORING!

WE PUT THOSE ERASERS AWAY **FAST**. BUT I'M GOING TO GET MORE AND MAKE A WHOLE ARMY NEXT TIME. OMAR WANTS TO MAKE ERASER ALIENS. I TOLD HIM WE CAN DO BOTH.

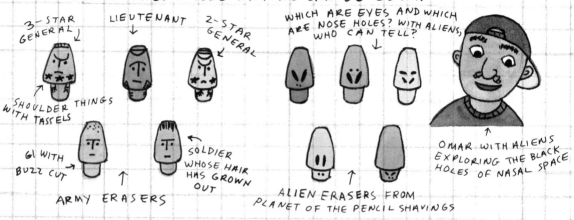

3-STAR GENERAL ↓

LIEUTENANT ↓

2-STAR GENERAL ↙

WHICH ARE EYES AND WHICH ARE NOSE HOLES? WITH ALIENS, WHO CAN TELL? ↓

↑ SHOULDER THINGS WITH TASSELS

GI WITH BUZZ CUT →

← SOLDIER WHOSE HAIR HAS GROWN OUT

ARMY ERASERS

ALIEN ERASERS FROM PLANET OF THE PENCIL SHAVINGS

↑ OMAR WITH ALIENS EXPLORING THE BLACK HOLES OF NASAL SPACE

I'M THINKING OF INVENTING A GAME USING THE ALIEN ERASERS. I WANT TO MAKE SOMETHING REALLY COOL THAT WE CAN SELL AND MAKE A LOT OF MONEY FROM. OMAR WANTS US TO MAKE A COMIC BOOK INSTEAD. HE'S ALREADY DRAWN THE FIRST PART.

I DREW THE REST. IT TURNED OUT PRETTY GOOD.

KEVIN READING WITH HEADPHONES
SURGICALLY ATTACHED TO HIS EARS →

AS BORING AS SCHOOL IS, SOME DAYS IT'S A <u>LOT</u> BETTER
THAN BEING AT HOME. KEVIN STAYS IN HIS ROOM WITH HIS
HEADPHONES ON, SO HE DOESN'T NOTICE, BUT I DO. I CAN'T
HELP BUT HEAR MOM AND DAD YELLING. LAST NIGHT
THERE WAS LOTS OF DOOR SLAMMING, TOO. THIS MORNING,
DAD HAD ALREADY GONE TO WORK WHEN I GOT UP, BUT I
COULD SEE FROM MOM'S SWOLLEN, RED EYES THAT SHE'D
BEEN CRYING.

I TRIED TO
CHEER HER UP.

GREAT
NEWS,
MOM!

I'M WORKING ON
AN INVENTION THAT
TURNS SAD, RED EYES
INTO CLEAR, HAPPY
EYES. I JUST NEED TO
FIGURE OUT ONE MORE
INGREDIENT TO FINISH
IT.

MOM WASN'T VERY EXCITED. SHE SAID SHE'D NEED MUCH
MORE THAN AN EYE OINTMENT TO CURE HER PROBLEM.
I WANTED TO ASK HER WHAT WOULD HELP AND WHY SHE
AND DAD ARE SO MAD AT EACH OTHER. BUT I DIDN'T.
I COULDN'T.

ERASER
MOM
↓

ERASER
DAD
↓

DO YOU EVER
<u>LISTEN</u> TO WHAT
I SAY?

WHY SHOULD I?
IT'S ALWAYS THE
SAME OLD THING.

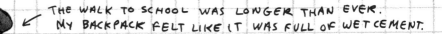

THE WALK TO SCHOOL WAS LONGER THAN EVER. MY BACKPACK FELT LIKE IT WAS FULL OF WET CEMENT.

OMAR COULD TELL SOMETHING WAS WRONG TODAY. HE ASKED ME IF I WAS SICK OR SOMETHING.

WHAT'S UP WITH YOU ANYWAY?

YOU'RE NOT PLAYING WITH YOUR ERASER ARMY UNDER YOUR DESK.

THAT'S NOT NORMAL!

I JUST DON'T FEEL LIKE IT.

YOU'RE NOT GONNA PUKE ARE YOU?

DON'T WORRY— I WON'T PUKE.

I DON'T WANT TO TALK ABOUT MOM AND DAD. NOT TO OMAR. BUT MAYBE KEVIN KNOWS WHAT'S GOING ON — I'LL ASK HIM TONIGHT. BUT FIRST I'D BETTER BE PREPARED. TALKING TO KEVIN CAN BE LIKE A VERY COMPLICATED EXPERIMENT. YOU'RE HOPING FOR A CERTAIN RESULT AND IN ORDER TO GET IT, CERTAIN SPECIAL STEPS MUST BE TAKEN.

MOM SAYS KEVIN IS SO TOUCHY BECAUSE OF HORMONES.

THOSE ARE THE SAME THINGS THAT GIVE HIM PIMPLES. I THINK GETTING UGLY BUMPS ALL OVER YOUR FACE IS REASON ENOUGH TO BE GROUCHY!

EXPERIMENT #5:
HOW TO GET MOODY, EASILY IRRITATED OLDER BROTHER IN THE MOOD TO TALK TO HIS BELOVED YOUNGER BROTHER

INGREDIENTS: ONE MUG OF HOT CHOCOLATE

 ONE PLATE OF COOKIES

 ONE (MAYBE TWO, BUT <u>NO</u> MORE) RESPECTFUL RAP ON THE DOOR

KNOCK KNOCK

1. WHEN DOOR IS OPEN A CRACK, QUICKLY OFFER THE HOT CHOCOLATE AND COOKIES. BROTHER SHOULD THEN ALLOW ACCESS TO HIS USUALLY FORBIDDEN ROOM.

2. WALK IN. PUT DOWN CUP AND PLATE (<u>NOT</u> NEAR THE COMPUTER OR SPEEDY EJECTION FROM ROOM WILL FOLLOW.)

3. ASK BROTHER <u>IN A SOFT VOICE</u> (VERY IMPORTANT — <u>DON'T</u> BE LOUD OR WHINY) IF YOU CAN TALK TO HIM FOR A MINUTE.

RESULTS: IT WORKED! KEVIN ACTUALLY LET ME IN HIS ROOM FOR FIVE MINUTES, BUT HE DIDN'T TELL ME MUCH, NOT WHAT I REALLY WANTED TO KNOW.

HE LOOKED AT THE COMPUTER, NOT AT ME.

HOW SHOULD I KNOW WHY MOM AND DAD FIGHT SO MUCH? MAYBE THEY DON'T LIKE EACH OTHER ANYMORE.

THAT WAS DEFINITELY **NOT** WHAT I WANTED TO HEAR. OMAR'S PARENTS ARE DIVORCED, SO I GUESS I COULD ASK HIM WHAT THE WARNING SIGNS ARE. BUT WHAT GOOD WOULD THAT DO? I DON'T WANT TO KNOW IF THEY **ARE** GETTING DIVORCED, I WANT TO **KEEP** THEM FROM DOING IT. I NEED TO INVENT A PREVENT-A-DIVORCE MACHINE. BUT WHAT WOULD THAT BE? WOULD IT BE SOME KIND OF ROBOT?

INVENTION #4:

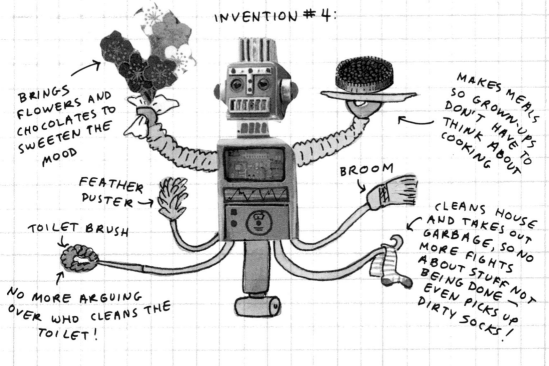

BRINGS FLOWERS AND CHOCOLATES TO SWEETEN THE MOOD

MAKES MEALS SO GROWN-UPS DON'T HAVE TO THINK ABOUT COOKING

FEATHER DUSTER →

BROOM

TOILET BRUSH

CLEANS HOUSE AND TAKES OUT GARBAGE, SO NO MORE FIGHTS ABOUT STUFF NOT BEING DONE — EVEN PICKS UP DIRTY SOCKS!

NO MORE ARGUING OVER WHO CLEANS THE TOILET!

OTHER ROBOT DESIGNS

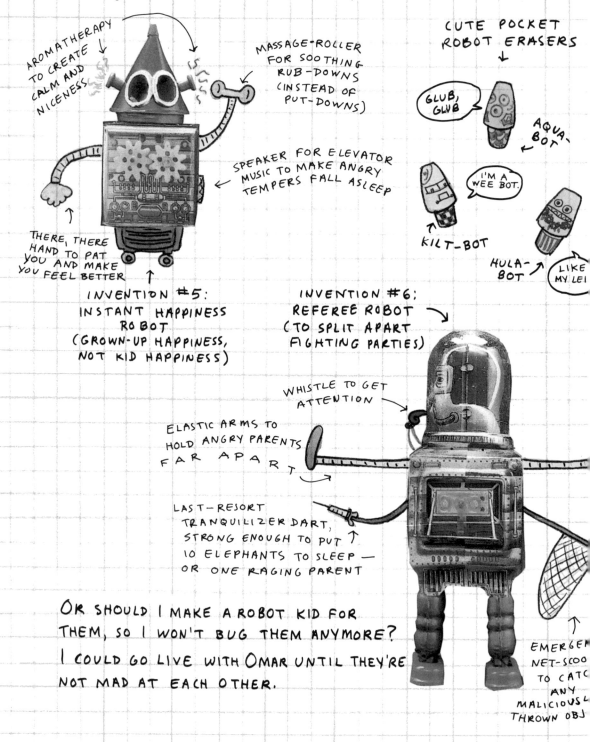

AROMATHERAPY TO CREATE CALM AND NICENESS ↓

MASSAGE-ROLLER FOR SOOTHING RUB-DOWNS (INSTEAD OF PUT-DOWNS)

SPEAKER FOR ELEVATOR MUSIC TO MAKE ANGRY TEMPERS FALL ASLEEP ←

THERE, THERE HAND TO PAT YOU AND MAKE YOU FEEL BETTER ↑

INVENTION #5: INSTANT HAPPINESS ROBOT (GROWN-UP HAPPINESS, NOT KID HAPPINESS)

CUTE POCKET ROBOT ERASERS ↓

GLUB, GLUB

AQUA-BOT

I'M A WEE BOT.

KILT-BOT

HULA-BOT →

LIKE MY LEI

INVENTION #6: REFEREE ROBOT (TO SPLIT APART FIGHTING PARTIES) ↘

WHISTLE TO GET ATTENTION

ELASTIC ARMS TO HOLD ANGRY PARENTS F A R   A P A R T ↘

LAST-RESORT TRANQUILIZER DART, STRONG ENOUGH TO PUT 10 ELEPHANTS TO SLEEP — OR ONE RAGING PARENT ↑

OR SHOULD I MAKE A ROBOT KID FOR THEM, SO I WON'T BUG THEM ANYMORE? I COULD GO LIVE WITH OMAR UNTIL THEY'RE NOT MAD AT EACH OTHER.

EMERGEN... NET-SCOO... TO CATC... ANY MALICIOUSL... THROWN OBJ...

MAYBE I'M WORRIED FOR NOTHING. DAD PROMISED TO TAKE ME TO HIS LAB TOMORROW AND SHOW ME WHAT HE'S WORKING ON. HE HASN'T DONE THAT IN A LONG TIME! MAYBE HE'S GOING TO BE A NORMAL DAD NOW AND DO MORE THINGS WITH US INSTEAD OF ALWAYS WORKING.

SINCE DAD WAS IN A GOOD MOOD, I WANTED HIM TO STAY THAT WAY. I THOUGHT HAVING HIS FAVORITE DINNER WOULD HELP. UNFORTUNATELY, MOM DIDN'T AGREE.

HEY, MOM, HOW ABOUT WE HAVE MEAT LOAF FOR DINNER? DAD LOVES THAT!

STEAM COMING OUT OF EARS

DO I LOVE RUNNING TO THE STORE AND HAVING MORE WORK TO DO?

WHEN MOM IS IN A BAD MOOD, SHE TAKES IT OUT ON FOOD.

I TELL MOM THAT IF YOU HAVE HAIR LIKE HERS, YOU SHOULDN'T WEAR POLKA DOTS OR YOU'LL LOOK LIKE A CLOWN. HERE SHE'S AN ANGRY CLOWN, A BAD COMBINATION.

MAYBE BECAUSE WE HAD STUPID SPAGHETTI, DAD BROKE HIS PROMISE. I KNOW IF WE'D HAD MEAT LOAF, THINGS WOULD HAVE BEEN DIFFERENT. I KNOW IT.

GLUED-TOGETHER SPAGHETTI (YOU CAN'T TWIRL THIS ON YOUR FORK — YOU HAVE TO SHOVEL)

LUMPY MASHED POTATOES (SMASHED POTATOES)

CRUNCHY UNDERCOOKED RICE (LIKE EATING PLASTIC)

CARBONIZED FISH STICK (MORE STICK THAN FISH)

PAD →

I'M SORRY, MAX, BUT SOMETHING'S COME UP. YOUR MOTHER AND I REALLY NEED TO TALK TODAY. WE'LL GO TO THE LAB ANOTHER DAY, I PROMISE.

IT'S A BAD SIGN WHEN A PARENT SAYS "YOUR MOTHER" OR "YOUR FATHER" INSTEAD OF "MOM" AND "DAD."

LIKE I DON'T KNOW WHAT A PROMISE FROM HIM IS WORTH NOW!

I DON'T KNOW WHY I BOTHERED WITH ROBOT PLANS — WHAT I REALLY NEED IS SOMETHING TO <u>MAKE</u> PEOPLE KEEP THEIR PROMISES.

INVENTION #7: ELECTRIC PROMISE PROD

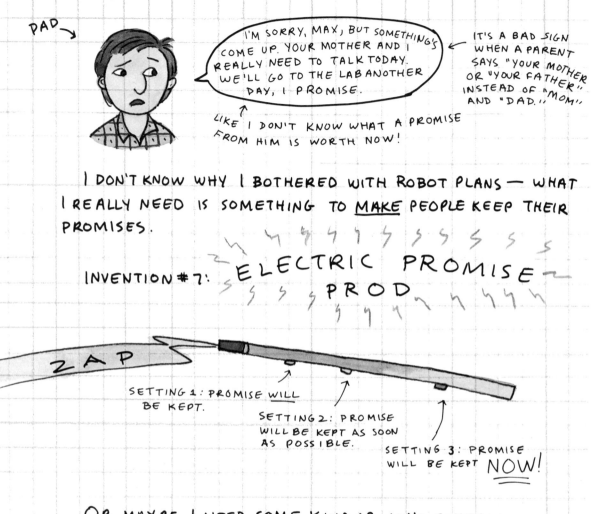

ZAP

SETTING 1: PROMISE WILL BE KEPT.

SETTING 2: PROMISE WILL BE KEPT AS SOON AS POSSIBLE.

SETTING 3: PROMISE WILL BE KEPT <u>NOW</u>!

OR MAYBE I NEED SOME KIND OF MIND CONTROL.

INVENTION #8: HYPNODISKS

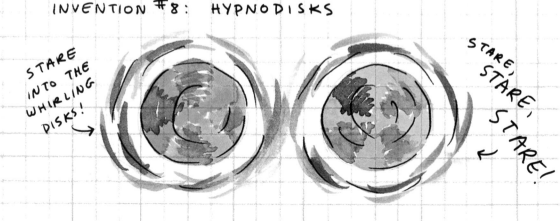

STARE INTO THE WHIRLING DISKS!

STARE, STARE, STARE!

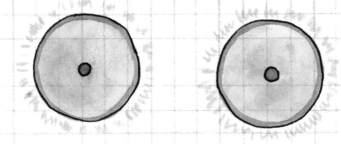

NOW FOCUS ON THE DOTS. THE DOTS ARE GOOD. THE DOTS ARE POWERFUL. YOU WILL DO AS THE DOTS SAY.

MAKE MEAT LOAF! ↓

TAKE ME TO YOUR LAB! ↓

ZOMBIE MOM

MEAT LOAF GOOD! MEAT LOAF YUM-YUM!

APRON — RARELY WORN

ONION   SPOON

LAB GOOD! LAB FUN! COME TO GOOD, FUN LAB!

CAR KEYS ↓

ZOMBIE DAD

MAGNETIC CARD TO GET INTO LAB

TOO BAD THIS WOULDN'T REALLY WORK. I CAN MAKE MY ARMY AND ALIEN ERASERS DO WHATEVER I WANT, BUT NOT MY PARENTS.

I HAVE SOME NEW ERASERS TO SHOW OMAR TOMORROW. THESE ARE THE BIG GUYS

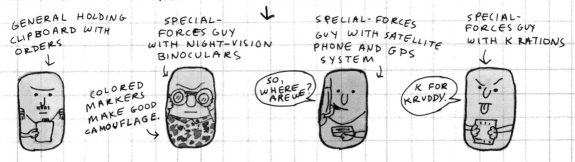

GENERAL HOLDING CLIPBOARD WITH ORDERS ↓

COLORED MARKERS MAKE GOOD CAMOUFLAGE. ↓

SPECIAL-FORCES GUY WITH NIGHT-VISION BINOCULARS ↓

SO, WHERE ARE WE?

SPECIAL-FORCES GUY WITH SATELLITE PHONE AND GPS SYSTEM ↓

K FOR KRUDDY.

SPECIAL-FORCES GUY WITH K RATIONS ↓

ALIEN BLOBS →

OMAR THOUGHT MY NEW ERASERS WERE REALLY COOL. HE WANTED TO MAKE ALIEN BLOBS LIKE THEM. WHILE HE WAS WORKING ON HIS FIRST ONE, I THOUGHT IT WAS A GOOD TIME TO ASK HIM.

I TOOK A DEEP BREATH. BEFORE I COULD CHANGE MY MIND, I SAID, "SO YOU DON'T MIND YOUR PARENTS BEING DIVORCED?"

HE DIDN'T SAY ANYTHING FOR A WHILE. THEN HE GRUNTED. A GOOD GRUNT? A BAD GRUNT? I WASN'T SURE.

"WEEELLL," HE FINALLY SAID, "IT'D BE BETTER IF THEY WERE STILL MARRIED... BUT NOT IF THEY WOULD FIGHT THE WAY THEY USED TO. MAN, IT GOT UGLY!"

DIVORCE WAS BETTER THAN FIGHTING? I'M NOT SO SURE. I CAN ALWAYS USE HEADPHONES LIKE KEVIN DOES TO BLOCK OUT YELLING AND DOOR-SLAMMING.

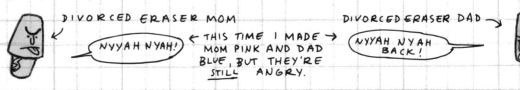

I'D RATHER MAKE COMICS WITH OMAR THAN TALK ABOUT DIVORCE ANYWAY.

EVIL-TEACHER → ERASERS

DETENTION!

CONFISCATION!

PAY ATTENTION!

NOT TO MENTION!

MS. BLODGE ALMOST CAUGHT US DRAWING ALIEN ERASER'S LATEST ADVENTURE. I DEFINITELY DON'T WANT HER TO CONFISCATE THAT! (BESIDES, IF SHE SEES THE WORD "FART," SHE'LL GIVE US DETENTION FOR SURE. SHE'S LIKE THAT.)

NOW PAY ATTENTION, CLASS! YES, OMAR, THAT MEANS YOU. AND YOU, TOO, MAX!

CLASS, TODAY WE HAVE A SPECIAL GUEST. MR. CABRILLO IS GOING TO TALK TO US ABOUT CONFLICT RESOLUTION — THAT'S A WAY OF WORKING TO AVOID FIGHTS.

THIS COULD BE JUST WHAT I NEED! IF I CAN GET MY PARENTS TO DO THIS CONFLICT-RESOLUTION STUFF INSTEAD OF FIGHTING, THEY WON'T GET DIVORCED!

MR. CABRILLO SMILED A LOT, LIKE IT'S SO MUCH FUN NOT TO FIGHT.

I'M NOT SURE HOW USEFUL HIS TIPS ARE. HE HAD SOME KIDS ACT OUT SITUATIONS THAT COULD HAVE STARTED FIGHTS BUT DIDN'T, LIKE ACCIDENTALLY ELBOWING SOMEBODY OR STEPPING ON SOMEONE'S LUNCH BY MISTAKE. THOSE AREN'T THE KINDS OF THINGS MOM AND DAD FIGHT ABOUT.

INSTEAD OF THIS

THIS

BAD! NO-NO! DON'T DO
IT THIS WAY!

GOOD! THAT'S THE IDEA!
TRY IT LIKE THIS!

ACTUALLY, I'M NOT SURE THIS STUFF WILL
WORK WITH KIDS, EITHER.

THEN HE HAD US WRITE A LIST OF FACTS ABOUT OURSELVES,
THINGS WE LIKE AND DON'T LIKE. HE MEANT WE SHOULD WRITE ABOUT
OTHER KIDS — NOT I LIKE JEFF AND I DON'T LIKE DAMIEN, BUT I LIKE
BEING INCLUDED AND I   DON'T LIKE BEING TEASED, STUFF
LIKE THAT.

REMEMBER, NO NAMES
PLEASE. AND NO
PERSONAL REMARKS.

BY THAT HE MEANT, DON'T SAY
"I DON'T LIKE HOW MARTY ALWAYS
PICKS HIS NOSE."

LIST OF GOOD/BAD STUFF

1. I LIKE INVENTING STUFF!
2. I LIKE DRAWING!
3. I LIKE BEING IN CONTROL!
4. I LIKE MAKING SOLDIERS AND ALIENS!
5. I LIKE BEING A BORN LEADER!
6. I LIKE MAKING COMICS WITH OMAR!
7. I LIKE WRITING EXCLAMATION POINTS !!!!!
8. I DON'T LIKE HEARING MY PARENTS FIGHT!
9. I DON'T LIKE BROKEN PROMISES!
10. I DON'T LIKE LISTENING TO BORING LECTURES!
11. I DON'T LIKE BEING SENT TO DETENTION!
12. I DON'T LIKE MY STUFF TO BE CONFISCATED!
13. I DON'T LIKE ACTING IN STUPID SKITS!
14. I DON'T LIKE WRITING LISTS!

← I DO LIKE ALL KINDS OF ROBOTS →

I HAVE NO IDEA HOW MAKING A LIST IS SUPPOSED TO KEEP YOU FROM FIGHTING, BUT AT LEAST MR. CABRILLO USED UP SO MUCH TIME, WE MISSED MATH FOR THE DAY.

MR. CABRILLO MIGHT NOT HAVE MEANT TO, BUT HE GAVE ME A
GREAT IDEA! I'LL MAKE AN INVENTION THAT WILL SHOW MOM AND
DAD HOW TO GET ALONG. AN INVENTION IS <u>MUCH</u> BETTER THAN THE
SKITS MR. CABRILLO HAD US DO TODAY. OR THE DUMB LISTS.

INVENTION #9:
GLITTER JAR →

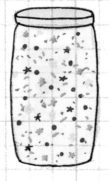

1. MIX RUBBING ALCOHOL WITH OIL.

2. ADD BEADS, SEQUINS, GLITTER, TINY
   SHINY THINGS.

3. ADD A <u>LITTLE</u> FOOD COLORING IF YOU
   WANT.

4. SHAKE THE JAR. THE OIL AND
   ALCOHOL DON'T MIX — THEY FIGHT—
   BUT TOGETHER THEY'RE VERY PRETTY.

OTHER KINDS OF JARS YOU CAN MAKE!

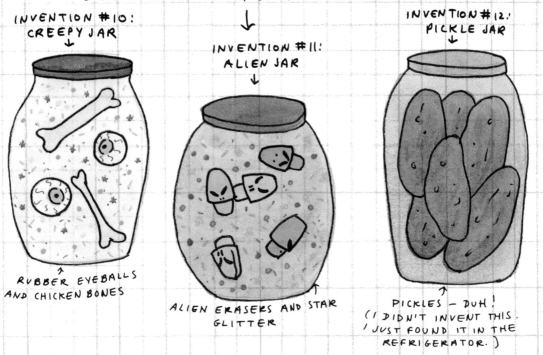

INVENTION #10:
CREEPY JAR
↓

INVENTION #11:
ALIEN JAR
↓

INVENTION #12:
PICKLE JAR
↓

RUBBER EYEBALLS
AND CHICKEN BONES

ALIEN ERASERS AND STAR
GLITTER

PICKLES — DUH!
(I DIDN'T INVENT THIS.
I JUST FOUND IT IN THE
REFRIGERATOR.)

IF YOU WANT PRETTY, NOT CREEPY, A SWIRL JAR IS GOOD. FILL
A JAR ABOUT 1/4 FULL OF DISH SOAP (ONE WITH GLYCOL STEARATE
IN IT), ADD A COUPLE DROPS OF FOOD COLORING, THEN TRICKLE
COLD WATER IN TO FILL UP JAR. CAP IT AND SWIRL!

INVENTION #13:
SWIRL-EE

WARNING!
DON'T PUT
IN WATER
TOO QUICKLY
OR YOU'LL
HAVE A JAR
OF FOAM!

I GAVE MOM AND DAD THE GLITTER JAR LAST NIGHT.
I TOLD THEM IT WAS A SCIENTIFIC EXAMPLE OF HOW TWO
THINGS (OIL AND ALCOHOL) CAN FIGHT BUT STILL WORK
TOGETHER TO MAKE SOMETHING REALLY COOL. I THOUGHT
SINCE THEY'RE BOTH SCIENTISTS, THEY'D GET WHAT I WAS
SAYING. INSTEAD THEY JUST LOOKED AT EACH OTHER IN A
VERY SAD WAY.

I GUESS THAT INVENTION'S A DUD.

TO MAKE UP FOR NOT LIKING MY GLITTER JAR (HE SAID
HE LIKED IT, BUT HE SURE DIDN'T LOOK HAPPY ABOUT IT),
DAD SHOWED ME A WATER EXPERIMENT. IT WAS FUN DOING
SOMETHING LIKE THAT TOGETHER, BUT IT WAS A SAD KIND
OF FUN BECAUSE NEITHER OF US WAS HAPPY.

EXPERIMENT #6: HOW DO HOT AND COLD WATER REACT
TO EACH OTHER?

1. FILL A JAR WITH HOT
WATER. ADD RED FOOD
COLORING.

2. FILL ANOTHER JAR
WITH COLD WATER.
ADD BLUE FOOD
COLORING.

3. SEAL THE TOP OF THE
RED JAR WITH A PIECE
OF CARDBOARD OR AN
INDEX CARD. (WATER
PRESSURE SHOULD HOLD
IT ON.)

4. QUICKLY FLIP
OVER THE RED
JAR ON TOP OF
THE BLUE JAR.

5. PULL AWAY
THE CARDBOARD
CAREFULLY.
(HOLD ON TO
THE JARS!)

6. WILL THE COLORS
MIX TOGETHER
AND BLEND INTO
PURPLE OR
STAY SEPARATE
AND FIGHT EACH
OTHER?

RESULTS:
BAD NEWS! THEY
FIGHT! THE COLORS
DON'T WANT TO MIX!

I SAID IT WAS A SAD
EXPERIMENT TO HAVE THE
COLORS SEPARATE LIKE THAT.
DAD SMILED AND SAID WE SHOULD
TRY IT THE OTHER WAY AROUND,
WITH THE BLUE JAR
ON TOP. SO WE DID.

AND THEY
MIXED! ⟶

BEAUTIFUL,
BEAUTIFUL
← PURPLE!

SO MAYBE THERE'S HOPE FOR NOT GETTING A DIVORCE
AFTER ALL. SOMETIMES YOU CAN FIGHT AND SOMETIMES JUST
THE OPPOSITE!

I DIDN'T TELL MOM AND DAD ABOUT MR. CABRILLO AND CONFLICT
RESOLUTION, BUT I TOLD KEVIN. HE SAID MR. CABRILLO HAD TALKED
TO HIS CLASS WHEN HE WAS
MY AGE.

DID HE HAVE YOU
DO THE SQUASHED-
LUNCH SKIT?

YEAH,
THE SAME
ONE.

THAT ONE
CRACKED ME
UP!

DO YOU
THINK IT
WORKS?

KEVIN SAID IT COULD WORK, BUT IT DEPENDS ON THE KIDS WANTING
IT TO WORK OUT. YOU HAVE TO WANT NOT TO FIGHT.

WHEN MOM KISSED ME GOOD NIGHT, SHE TOLD ME NOT TO WORRY.
I WAS AFRAID TO ASK WHAT IT IS I'M NOT SUPPOSED TO WORRY
ABOUT. INSTEAD I JUST LAY THERE IN THE DARK — WORRYING.

WHY DO THINGS ALWAYS SEEM WORSE IN THE MIDDLE OF THE NIGHT? STOMACHACHES HURT TWICE AS MUCH, NOISES ARE 10 TIMES SCARIER, AND SMALL WORRIES GET BIGGER AND BIGGER INSTEAD OF GOING AWAY. AND WHY DO WE WORRY ANYWAY? IT'S NOT USEFUL — THINGS DON'T GET BETTER FROM WORRYING ABOUT THEM. YOU'D THINK WE'D LOSE WORRYING AS WE EVOLVED, LIKE WE LOST HAVING A TAIL.

BLACK CLOUDS OF WORRIES

↓

Now I KNOW I HAVE SOMETHING TO WORRY ABOUT.
MOM AND DAD CALLED A FAMILY MEETING FOR TONIGHT.
WE HAVEN'T HAD A FAMILY MEETING SINCE I ACCIDENTALLY
BROKE THE KITCHEN WINDOW. IT'S GOT TO BE
SOMETHING SERIOUS.

I TRIED TO EAT DINNER, BUT THE MEATBALLS FELT LIKE LEAD BALLS.

THE APPLESAUCE WAS LIKE CEMENT, AND THE RICE TASTED LIKE GRITTY SAND.

IT WASN'T A MEAL, IT WAS CONSTRUCTION MATERIAL.

I COULD TELL MOM AND DAD WERE NERVOUS. KEVIN
LOOKED NERVOUS, TOO. THEIR NERVOUSNESS MADE ME
EVEN MORE NERVOUS. THE AIR IN THE ROOM FELT LIKE
A RUBBER BAND THAT HAD BEEN S T R E T C H E D
TIGHT AND WAS ABOUT TO SNAP.

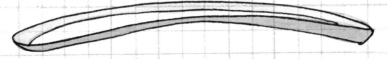

AND THEN THE SNAP CAME — MOM SAID WE MUST
HAVE NOTICED SOME TENSION BETWEEN HER AND DAD
(KEVIN AND I SAID NOTHING) AND THEY HAD DECIDED IT
WOULD BE BETTER FOR THEM TO SEPARATE.

DAD SAID HE'D ALREADY FOUND AN APARTMENT AND WOULD MOVE OUT THIS WEEKEND. WE'RE SUPPOSED TO STAY WITH MOM DURING THE WEEK AND EVERY OTHER WEEKEND WE'LL STAY WITH DAD.

DAD TRIED TO BE NICE ABOUT IT. "WE'RE STILL A FAMILY," HE SAID. "I'LL ALWAYS BE YOUR DAD." BUT THAT'S NOT MY IDEA OF A FAMILY, NOT MY IDEA OF A DAD.

THEN WE HAD A STIFF FAMILY HUG.

A HUG WHERE MOM AND DAD WERE VERY CAREFUL NOT TO TOUCH EACH OTHER AT ALL.

DAD LOOKED MISERABLE.

KEVIN STARED STRAIGHT AHEAD, HIS FACE A BLANK.

ME, I DIDN'T KNOW WHERE TO LOOK OR WHAT TO FEEL.

MOM LOOKED AT THE FLOOR.

IT WAS THE WORST NIGHT OF MY LIFE.

BLACK CLOUDS OF WORRY TURNED TO BLACK CLOUDS OF DOOM.

YOU WOULD THINK SOMEONE LEAVING YOUR FAMILY
WOULD LEAVE A BIG HOLE IN THE MIDDLE OF THE HOUSE,
BUT DAD ONLY TOOK HIS STUFF AND LEFT EVERYTHING
ELSE THE SAME. EXCEPT FOR LITTLE THINGS.
DAD HUGGED US GOOD-BYE AND HE WAS GONE.

NO MORE CRACKED
COFFEE CUP THAT NO
ONE DARED WASH BECAUSE
DAD LIKES THE TASTE OF
OLD GRIMY COFFEE
MIXED WITH FRESH
COFFEE
↓

NO MORE WEIGHTS IN
THE LIVING ROOM TO
PLAY WITH WHILE
WATCHING MOVIES.
↓

MOM USED TO JOKE THAT
WHEN DAD DRANK FROM THIS
CUP, HE TASTED EVERY CUP OF
COFFEE HE'D EVER MADE.
I GUESS SHE WON'T
MAKE THAT JOKE AGAIN.
↑

NOW HOW WILL I GET
STRONG?
↑

LET ME
EAT TOKYO
NOW!

NO MORE EXTRA-
LARGE RUBBER BOOTS
TO STOMP AROUND IN
PRETENDING TO BE →
GODZILLA

THIS MORNING EVERYTHING SEEMED WEIRDLY NORMAL, EXCEPT DAD WASN'T THERE (BUT HE OFTEN LEAVES FOR WORK REALLY EARLY). IT WAS LIKE BEING IN A "WHAT'S WRONG WITH THIS PICTURE" WHERE AT FIRST YOU CAN'T TELL THAT ANYTHING IS WRONG. BUT IF YOU LOOK CLOSELY...

INVENTION #14:
FRANKENSTEIN DAD MADE OF OLD, LEFTOVER DADS

NEED-A-HAIRCUT-DAD HAIR

STUBBLE-DAD FACE

PLAID-PANTS-DAD LEGS

BUSINESSMAN-DAD FEET WITH BUSINESS-TYPE SHOES

SOCCER-COACH-DAD CHEST (WITH WHISTLE)

I WAS THINKING I SHOULD TRY INVENTING A ROBOT DAD, ONE EVEN BETTER THAN THE REAL DAD, BUT I DON'T HAVE THE RIGHT PARTS, AND IT'S TOO COMPLICATED. OR INSTEAD OF A MOUSETRAP, I COULD INVENT A DAD TRAP, SO HE'D BE CAUGHT AND HAVE TO STAY.

INVENTION #15:
DAD TRAP

CHOCOLATE-BAR BAIT — DAD LOVES CHOCOLATE

DAD REACHES FOR CANDY, NOOSE TIGHTENS AROUND WRIST, AND — TA DA! — HE'S CAUGHT CHOCOLATE-HANDED!

IF I'M GOING TO BE TRAPPED HERE, CAN YOU AT LEAST BRING ME A GLASS OF MILK?

I THOUGHT MOM WOULD BE IN A BETTER MOOD WITH DAD GONE, BUT SHE WASN'T. SHE WAS AS CRABBY AS EVER. MAYBE SHE'S THE ONE WHO NEEDS CHOCOLATE, TO SWEETEN HER UP.

I WANTED TO TELL OMAR WHAT WAS WRONG, BUT I COULDN'T.
MAYBE IF NOBODY KNOWS MY DAD HAS MOVED OUT, IT HASN'T
REALLY HAPPENED. MAYBE I IMAGINED THE WHOLE THING.
MAYBE I'VE INVENTED SOME WEIRD ALTERNATIVE REALITY I'M
STUCK IN. MAYBE.

OMAR LINED UP HIS ALIEN ERASERS, AND I TRIED TO PLAY
WITH HIM, BUT HE COULD TELL I WASN'T REALLY PAYING ATTENTION.

MY DRAWINGS OF HANDS LOOK LIKE ALIENS!

THEN CLASS STARTED AND THINGS GOT WORSE. MS. BLODGE WAS
MAD I HADN'T TURNED IN MY HOMEWORK (YEAH, YEAH, I FORGOT IT),
AND SHE SAID I'D HAVE TO STAY INSIDE DURING RECESS TO FINISH IT.
SO I STAYED INSIDE. BUT I DIDN'T DO MY HOMEWORK. I WORKED
ON THE COMIC INSTEAD.

MOM GOT HOT CHOCOLATE AND DOUGHNUTS FOR KEVIN AND
ME AFTER SCHOOL. SHE'S NEVER DONE THAT BEFORE. THEN I DID
MY HOMEWORK (YES, MS. BLODGE, ALL OF IT!) BEFORE DAD
CAME TO TAKE ME AND KEVIN OUT FOR PIZZA.

IT'S LIKE BOTH MOM AND DAD ARE BEING NICE WITH FOOD BECAUSE
IT'S THE ONLY WAY THEY CAN BE NICE RIGHT NOW.

↓

SWEET DOUGHNUT-
TOO SWEET AND DOUGHY
TODAY

PEPPERONI PIZZA - USUALLY MY
FAVORITE, BUT IT DIDN'T TASTE RIGHT
SOMEHOW

WE ATE PIZZA AND TOLD BAD JOKES AND THINGS ALMOST
FELT NORMAL. ALMOST, I KEPT TELLING MYSELF. UNTIL DAD
DROPPED US BACK AT THE HOUSE LIKE HE'D JUST BEEN
GIVING US A RIDE AND WASN'T PART OF OUR FAMILY, REALLY.
THERE WAS NO PRETENDING NORMAL THEN, AND THINGS GOT
REALLY WEIRD. DAD HUGGED KEVIN AND ME, AND I COULD
SEE HE WAS CRYING.

SO I WHISPERED IN HIS EAR, "DON'T WORRY, DAD, WE'LL
INVENT ANOTHER KIND OF FAMILY." AND WE WILL. I KNOW
WE WILL.

IF YOU TAKE APART A FAMILY, CAN YOU PUT IT BACK TOGETHER
IN A WAY THAT MAKES SENSE?

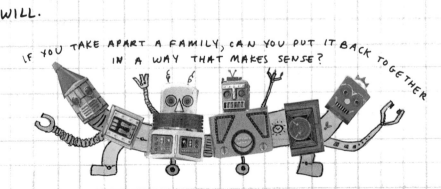

I'M JUST NOT SURE <u>WHAT</u> KIND OF FAMILY WE'LL BE. A FAMILY WITH A PART-TIME DAD? A HALF OF A FAMILY? A FAMILY AND A HALF? A SMEARED-UP MISTAKE OF A FAMILY THAT I WISH I COULD ERASE AND REDRAW?

OR IS THE DAD ALREADY ERASED CLEAN OUT OF THE FAMILY PICTURE?
↓

AM I THE ONLY ONE WHO NOTICES <u>SOMEONE</u> IS MISSING? ↑

WHEN I FIGURE OUT WHAT FAMILY WE ARE NOW, THEN I GUESS I CAN DRAW A NEW PICTURE OF US. OR ERASE A NEW ONE.

IF <u>I</u> WAS AN ERASER, I WONDER WHAT KIND I'D BE. NOT THE GRUBBY, SMEARY KIND, I HOPE.

ERASER BOY →

HELP! THE MORE MISTAKES I MAKE, THE SMALLER I GET.

I'M SHRIIIIIIIIIINKING!

I GUESS I'M KIND OF GETTING USED TO DAD BEING GONE. MOM SAYS HE WAS NEVER HERE TO BEGIN WITH, BUT THAT'S NOT TRUE. WE STILL HAVEN'T STAYED AT HIS APARTMENT. WE HAVEN'T EVEN SEEN IT, BUT DAD SAYS AS SOON AS HE GETS THINGS FIXED UP, HE'LL HAVE KEVIN AND ME OVER.

I WONDER WHAT IT'LL BE LIKE. MAYBE DAD'S APARTMENT IS AN ALIEN WORLD.

MAP OF DAD ZONE (OR APARTMENT)

BLOOP

BLOOP

ALIEN LAVA PITS IN DAD'S KITCHEN

BURNT TOAST CRUSTS — PROOF THAT DAD WAS HERE

EXTRATERRESTRIAL SINGLE-SOCK AREA

DARK, MYSTERIOUS PLACE WHERE DAD CLAIMS ALL HIS SOCKS RUN AWAY TO

INTERGALACTIC FETID STINK PILE

GROSS STUFF DAD SWEARS IS GOOD FOR HOUSEPLANTS (BUT WHAT ABOUT US WHO HAVE NOSES?)

MOUNTAIN OF SHAVING STUBBLE

EVIDENCE OF OTHER LIFE FORMS EXISTING IN THE UNIVERSE

TOILET PAPER ROLL DESERT WASTELAND

SIGNS OF AN ALIEN ABDUCTION?

DAD'S PLACE WASN'T WHAT I'D IMAGINED. IT WAS SMALL
AND MOSTLY EMPTY, LIKE A DOCTOR'S WAITING ROOM —
NO SOCKS ANYWHERE THAT I COULD SEE. WE PLAYED
CARDS AND ATE POPCORN, BUT EVEN THAT DIDN'T MAKE IT
FEEL COZIER.

AFTER DAD WENT TO BED, KEVIN AND I STAYED UP TALKING.

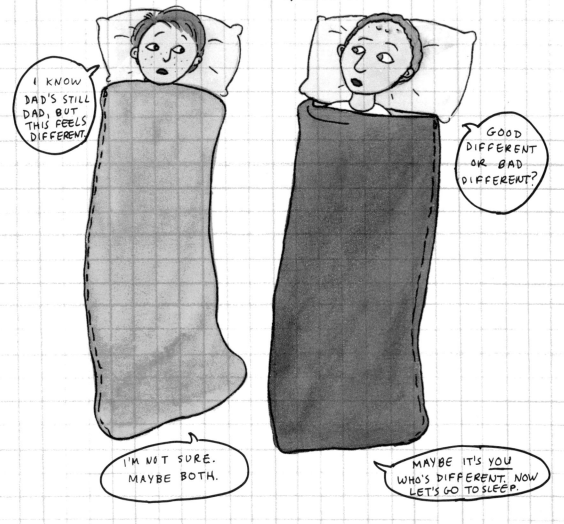

I KNOW DAD'S STILL DAD, BUT THIS FEELS DIFFERENT.

GOOD DIFFERENT OR BAD DIFFERENT?

I'M NOT SURE. MAYBE BOTH.

MAYBE IT'S YOU WHO'S DIFFERENT. NOW LET'S GO TO SLEEP.

THEN I HAD THE WEIRDEST DREAM.

POUGHNUT PLANET

LAVA PLANET

FINGERPRINT PLANET

WRINKLE PLANET

ALL MY ALIEN ERASERS WERE ALIVE, AND THEY WERE SHOWING ME THEIR PLANETS. IT WAS A GALACTIC TOUR, KIND OF. EACH PLACE WAS COOL IN A DIFFERENT WAY.

PINEAPPLE PLANET

HAPPY FACE PLANET

PUMPKIN PLANET

SPIKEY PLANET

ROTTEN PLANET

THEN I CAME TO A PLANET THAT WAS PERFECT FOR ME, FULL OF INVENTIONS AND EXPERIMENTAL STUFF. AND I KNEW THAT WAS WHERE I BELONGED. IN FRONT OF ME, I SAW TWO DOORS.

ONE LED TO MY BEDROOM.

THE OTHER OPENED INTO DAD'S NEW APARTMENT.

I WASN'T SURE WHICH DOOR TO GO THROUGH. DID I HAVE TO CHOOSE ONE OR THE OTHER? I COULDN'T DECIDE. A VOICE SUDDENLY BOOMED OUT.

To Elias,
the inspiration for it all,
and to the memory of Harvey, his wonderful father,
who will live within us always.

Published by Scholastic Press, a division of Scholastic Inc., Publishers since 1920.
Scholastic, Scholastic Press, and associated logos are trademarks
and/or registered trademarks of Scholastic Inc.

Library of Congress Cataloging-in-Publication Data
Moss, Marissa
Max's Logbook / by Marissa Moss — 1st ed.
p. cm.
Summary: Max's logbook of observations, drawings, experiments, and
inventions reveals the rich world of his imagination and
his feelings about his parents' divorce.
ISBN 0-439-46660-1
[1. Divorce—Fiction. 2. Imagination—Fiction. 3. Diaries—Fiction.] I. Title
PZ7.M8535 MAX 2003
[Fic]—dc21
2002070620

10 9 8 7 6 5 4 3 2 1   03 04 05 06 07
Printed in Singapore 46   First Edition, July 2003

The artwork for this book was created with colored pencil, gouache,
watercolor, ink, and collage.
No erasers or aliens were harmed in the making of this book.
(But a couple of robots got dented.)

Book design and hand-lettering (phew!)
by Marissa Moss